No No Square

Written By Jaf'Colby'E Kirvin
Illustrated By StallionStudios88

First paperback edition 2021

Book written by Jai'Colby'E Kirvin
Cover and Illustrations by StallionStudios88

ISBN 978-1-66780-363-0

Published by BookBaby
www.BookBaby.com

Dear Parents/Guardians:

As a child, I didn't know that being touched on by others and touching on others was a bad thing. I have suffered due to the lack of awarness that could have prevented so much trauma. As a man today, I know the impact of educating children about the danger of being touched by not only strangers, but also by family members, classmates, older kids, and more who we would never think about.

This book was wrtten to help you educate your child about the importance of saying no, and that it's ok to come to you about things like this.

From behind a bush, a monster saw Maya and Kobe playing at the park.

"NO!" yelled Kobe and Maya.

"Aww" said the monster sadly. "Well can I touch you?" asked the monster.

"NO, NO! You can't touch me there! You can't touch me anywhere! You can't touch me on my NO NO SQUARE."
Kobe and Maya yelled to the monster scaring him.

The monster got so scared after the kids yelled at him, he ran away as quickly as he could.

Maya and Kobe ran to their dad to tell him what happened while they were playing.

"Thank you for telling me and remember to always say no," their dad said as he hugged them.

One day at school, a little monster saw Kobe playing with his friend, Noah.

The monster got so scared she started to cry. The teacher noticed and walked over to see what was going on.

"Thank you for telling me and saying no," the teacher told Kobe as she hugged him.

Later that night it was family night at Maya and Kobe's house. Their cousins came over with their parents to eat and play games.

While in the living room with her family, Maya noticed that there was a missing controller.

While Maya looked for the controller, a monster peeked into her room.

The monster got so scared, he ran away as quickly as he could.

Maya ran to her dad as fast as she could and told him "Uncle tried to touch me."

"Thank you for telling me Maya." her dad said. "Always tell an adult and say no." he told her as he gave her a big hug.

THE END

Thank you for getting No No Square and congratulations on taking this step in speaking about this difficult topic with your child that so many parents don't consider. If you don't mind doing 2 THINGS:

1. Please leave me a review about the book

2. Send a picture to my instagram @jaicolbye with your child holding No No Square and I'll post it